1914

CANDLELIGHT FOR
Rebecca

By JACQUELINE DEMBAR GREENE

ILLUSTRATIONS ROBERT HUNT

VIGNETTES SUSAN MCALILEY

★ American Girl®

THE AMERICAN GIRLS

KAYA, an adventurous Nez Perce girl whose deep love for horses and respect for nature nourish her spirit

1774

FELICITY, a spunky, spritely colonial girl, full of energy and independence

1824

JOSEFINA, a Hispanic girl whose heart and hopes are as big as the New Mexico sky

1854

KIRSTEN, a pioneer girl of strength and spirit who settles on the frontier

1864

ADDY, a courageous girl determined to be free in the midst of the Civil War

1904  SAMANTHA, a bright Victorian beauty, an orphan raised by her wealthy grandmother

1914  REBECCA, a lively girl with dramatic flair growing up in New York City

1934  KIT, a clever, resourceful girl facing the Great Depression with spirit and determination

1944  MOLLY, who schemes and dreams on the home front during World War Two

1974  JULIE, a fun-loving girl from San Francisco who faces big changes—and creates a few of her own

Published by American Girl Publishing, Inc.
Copyright © 2009 by American Girl, LLC

Questions or comments? Call 1-800-845-0005, visit **americangirl.com**,
or write to Customer Service, American Girl, 8400 Fairway Place,
Middleton, WI 53562-0497.

Printed in China
09 10 11 12 13 14 LEO 10 9 8 7 6 5 4 3 2 1

PICTURE CREDITS
The following individuals and organizations have generously
given permission to reprint images contained in "Looking Back":
pp. 69–71—from *In the Month of Kislev* by Nina Jaffe, illustrated by Louise August, illustrations
copyright © 1992 by Louise August. Used by permission of Viking Penguin, a division of
Penguin Young Readers Group, a member of Penguin Group (USA) Inc., 345 Hudson St.,
New York, NY 10014. All rights reserved (Hanukkah scene); *The City's Christmas Tree, 1913*,
Madison Square Park, by Carlton Moorepark, Museum of the City of New York Print Archives;
Miriam and Ira D. Wallach Division of Art, Prints, and Photographs, The New York Public
Library/Art Resource (classroom Christmas tree); pp. 72–73—YIVO Institute for Jewish Research,
15 West 16th St., New York, NY 10011-6301 (children receiving coins); pp. 74–75—Statue of
Liberty Hanukkah Lamp maker: Manfred Anson, New Jersey, 1985, bronze, cast. Museum
purchase with Project Americana funds provided by Peachy and Mark Levy (HUCSM 27.154)
from the HUC Skirball Cultural Center Museum Collection, Los Angeles CA. Photography
by Susan Einstein; © Charles Gupton/Corbis (girl and mom lighting menorah).

Cataloging-in-Publication Data available from Library of Congress

TO MY AUNTS AND UNCLES,
WHO MADE EVERY HOLIDAY MEMORABLE

Rebecca's parents and grandparents came to America before Rebecca was born, along with millions of other Jewish immigrants from different parts of the world. These immigrants brought with them many different traditions and ways of being Jewish. Practices varied widely between families, and differences among Jewish families were just as common in Rebecca's time as they are today. Rebecca's stories show the way one Jewish family could have lived in 1914 and 1915.

Rebecca's grandparents spoke mostly *Yiddish,* a language that was common among Jews from Eastern Europe. For help in pronouncing or understanding the foreign words in this book, look in the glossary on page 76.

Table of Contents

Rebecca's Family and Friends

Rebecca's Family

PAPA
Rebecca's father, an understanding man who owns a small shoe store

MAMA
Rebecca's mother, who keeps a good Jewish home—and a good sense of humor

REBECCA
A lively girl who dreams of becoming an actress

SADIE AND SOPHIE
Rebecca's twin sisters, who like to remind Rebecca that they are fourteen

BENNY AND VICTOR
Rebecca's brothers, who are five and twelve

GRANDPA
*Rebecca's grandfather,
an immigrant from
Russia who carries on
the Jewish traditions*

BUBBIE
*Rebecca's grandmother,
an immigrant from
Russia who is feisty
and outspoken*

ROSE
*A girl in Rebecca's class
who knows what it's like
to be an immigrant*

MR. ROSSI
*Rebecca's grouchy
neighbor who lives in the
basement apartment*

CHAPTER
ONE
—

A HOLIDAY
PROJECT

Rebecca Rubin and her friend Rose Krensky pushed against a biting wind as they made their way to school. Most of the shops were still closed, and the streets were quieter than usual. Not many people wanted to be out in such cold weather.

"I'm freezing," Rebecca said. She draped her scarf across her nose.

"I have goosebumples," Rose complained.

Rebecca giggled. "You mixed up two words, but I like it. I have goosebumples, too."

The air held a hint of snow, and Rebecca felt a shiver of excitement. Winter weather meant it was almost time for Hanukkah, her favorite holiday.

All around, Rebecca saw Christmas decorations. "It seems like everything is red and green," she said to Rose. Store windows were framed in pine boughs, and some displayed miniature trees decorated with shiny glass balls and glittering ropes of tinsel. The doors on many of the row houses had pine wreaths with bright red ribbons. It seemed as if the entire neighborhood had changed from its drab everyday clothes into its best holiday outfit.

"I love seeing the candles in our *menorah*," Rebecca said, "but there really aren't any special decorations for Hanukkah, are there?"

"Sure there are," Rose replied with a sly smile. "We decorate our plates with *latkes*, and then we eat them!"

Rebecca could almost smell the crisply fried potato pancakes. "My mother's been buying potatoes by the bagful," she said. "We're going to make tons of latkes. My cousin Ana and her family are coming over on Friday night to celebrate the first night of Hanukkah. I can hardly wait!"

latkes

Best of all, Rebecca was going to wear her holiday dress. She had only worn it for Jewish New

Year services in the fall, and then Mama had put it away to save for other special occasions. The dress had an overskirt with scalloped edges that made Rebecca feel as if she were wearing flower petals. It would be a Hanukkah treat just to wear it again.

When they arrived at the schoolyard, Rebecca and Rose hopped up and down, trying to stay warm. As soon as Miss Maloney rang her big brass bell, they hurried into the classroom. The radiators hissed, but the room was so cold that Rebecca hated to take off her coat and wool scarf. She rubbed her hands together briskly before she folded them on the desk in front of her.

"Let's warm up a bit," Miss Maloney said. "Stand up, everyone." She led the students as they stretched beside their desks, reaching high toward the ceiling. "Inhale," Miss Maloney said. As they bent over to touch their toes, she directed, "Exhale! Let's get our blood circulating." The room began to warm up, and a thin layer of moisture fogged the windows. The children took deep breaths in and out and moved their arms in little circles, but when Rebecca sat down again, her feet were still freezing.

Miss Maloney placed a wooden crate on her desk. "Since it's almost Christmas," she said, "we are going to make a lovely gift for you to take home to your families." From the box she pulled a bright table decoration. A tall red candle rose from a base of greenery and berries. The fresh scent of pine wafted through the air.

"*Oooh!*" the students exclaimed in admiration.

"I made this centerpiece to show you what yours will look like," Miss Maloney explained. "I have collected all the materials we need." She pointed to the boughs that seemed to sprout from the base of the decoration. "The city allowed me to gather these fresh branches of balsam and pine in Central Park. The berries came from wild rose bushes." Clusters of dried red berries were nestled in the greenery, along with small pinecones. A vivid red bow added a cheerful finishing touch.

Rebecca gulped. They were going to make Christmas decorations! She glanced over at Rose, who wrinkled her forehead doubtfully.

"It's beautiful," sighed Lucy Valenti.

Miss Maloney pointed with pride to the tall red

candle that stood in the center of the decoration. "These candles were generously donated to us by Mr. O'Hara at the candy store near my apartment. Next week we will all write thank-you letters to him in our best handwriting, using pen and ink." Some of the boys groaned.

Rose raised her hand and stood stiffly by her desk when Miss Maloney called on her. "Excuse me," Rose said, "but at our house, we don't celebrate Christmas."

Miss Maloney smiled kindly, as if Rose simply didn't understand. "Christmas is a national holiday,

children, celebrated by Americans all over the
country. At the Capitol in Washington, D.C.,
there's even a decorated Christmas tree
for everyone to enjoy."

Rose opened her mouth as if to
argue, but then clamped it shut and
sat down without another word.

the Capitol

The teacher set out round wooden disks to
use as bases, along with pots of glue and pairs of
scissors. She pulled baskets of green boughs from
behind her desk and set out an assortment of
pinecones, berries, and rolls of wide ribbon. She
carefully unrolled a paper packet filled
with candles.

"There are just enough candles for
each of you to have one," she cautioned,
"so work carefully. If you break your
candle, it can't be replaced."

Rebecca wondered if it was true that the entire
country celebrated Christmas. Her family didn't.
She looked around the room. Her friend Gertie
Lowenstein was Jewish, and she was busily gathering
greenery for her centerpiece. In fact, everyone in the
class buzzed excitedly, except for Rose and Rebecca.

6

Miss Maloney handed Rebecca a wooden base and a red candle, and Rebecca took them reluctantly. Would it be wrong to do this school project? The other students had already set to work. And the centerpiece *was* beautiful. Rebecca hesitated for a moment, and then she had an idea about how to design hers.

She glued the candle carefully just off center. Then she selected several full branches to use around the base. She piled the boughs high and sniffed the piney scent that lingered on her fingers as she worked. The greenery smelled wonderful, almost spicy.

Yet an uneasy feeling nagged at her. She glanced over at Rose, who was frowning as she glued her candle to the base. Rose looked up and shrugged her shoulders, as if to say, *What can we do?*

Rebecca was still thinking about the project when she walked home from school. Frozen grass crunched under her feet as she took a shortcut across Tompkins Square Park. Even though Rebecca saw Christmas decorations on many of the buildings, she knew that was just on the outside. Inside the row houses and tenements in her neighborhood, most of the families were getting ready to celebrate Hanukkah.

Was Miss Maloney right that Christmas was a national holiday? It was true that stores and offices in most parts of New York City were closed on December 25. But on the Lower East Side, where Rebecca lived, peddlers would be selling their wares from carts as they did every day, warming their hands over small coal stoves. The candy store, the fish shop, and the delicatessen would be open as usual. Papa and Grandpa would go to work at the shoe store.

As she walked down the street to her own building, Rebecca looked up to see Hanukkah menorahs standing in many windows. The nine-branched candelabras were of different designs in gleaming silver or golden brass. Miss Maloney's greenery and red candles just wouldn't seem right in Jewish homes.

Rebecca was so lost in thought that she nearly bumped into Mr. Rossi, the janitor, who was sniffling as he swept the front steps.

"*Aah-choo!*" he sneezed, pulling a handkerchief from his pocket. He blew his nose with a noisy *honk!*

"Bless you," Rebecca said politely.

Mr. Rossi only grumbled. "I'm feeling sicker by the minute. I gotta get to bed." He frowned up at the dark clouds overhead. "How can I shovel these steps if it snows? How am I gonna take care of the birds?" His eyes were red and watery. "And now the cat is gone. She'll freeze if she's lost outside. I can't go looking for her and maybe get sicker."

Rebecca was always amazed that grouchy old Mr. Rossi looked after Pasta, the cat, and kept gentle pigeons in cages on the roof of the building. She went up to the rooftop often to talk to the birds and stroke their soft feathers. But Mr. Rossi chased the children away if he caught them on the roof.

"I'll keep an eye out for Pasta," Rebecca said. "And you shouldn't go out on the roof if you're sick. Maybe I could feed the pigeons for you." Mr. Rossi couldn't shoo her off if she was helping him!

The janitor turned away with a fit of coughing,

dragging the broom down the steps to his basement apartment. Rebecca noticed that his window was dark, and there were no holiday decorations anywhere, not even a paper snowflake. Just before he opened his door, he muttered, "If you're feeding my birds, you gotta be here before supper. Those birds need to eat to stay warm."

Rebecca skipped up the stairs and searched the hallway on each landing, but there was no sign of Pasta. The cat could be as cranky as Mr. Rossi, but Rebecca loved the pigeons—and now she was going to take care of them herself.

Inside the warm kitchen, Rebecca's sister Sadie was polishing the family's Hanukkah menorah. Sophie, Sadie's twin, stood by holding a dish towel.

"Mr. Rossi's sick, so I'm going to take care of his pigeons," Rebecca exclaimed. "I am filled with unbounded joy."

"You're filled with *what?*" Sadie asked.

"Unbounded joy," Rebecca repeated. "That's how the Rebecca in this story feels when something wonderful happens." She held up her latest book, *Rebecca of Sunnybrook Farm*. It was the best book she had ever

10

"Mr. Rossi's sick, so I'm going to take care of his pigeons,"
Rebecca exclaimed. "I am filled with unbounded joy."

11

checked out of the library. She had read dozens of books, but none of the characters was as interesting as Rebecca Randall.

Sophie buffed the menorah until it gleamed and then set it on the windowsill in the parlor. Sadie put two candles in their proper places.

"I suppose you'll also be filled with joy when you light the Hanukkah candles. You're still not old enough to light the Sabbath candles," Sadie taunted, "but even little Benny gets to light candles for Hanukkah." She whispered something to Sophie, and the twins went off to the bedroom and closed the door.

Rebecca bristled. She hated the way her sisters acted so grown-up all the time. Just because they were allowed to light the Sabbath candles every Friday night, they treated her like a baby. Rebecca hoped Mama would let her light candles someday soon. She dreamed of having candlesticks of her own and standing beside her sisters to light Sabbath candles, too.

Happily, Hanukkah was one holiday when even the youngest in the family had a turn to kindle the lights. The menorah held nine colorful wax candles—one for each of the eight nights of the holiday and a head candle, called the *shammas*, that was used to light the others. On the first night, Papa lit the shammas, and the youngest child held it to the wick of the first candle. That was always Benny's turn. Then each night of Hanukkah, one additional candle was added to the menorah, and Rebecca always had the second turn. Every night of the holiday, they added one more candle until all nine burned brightly. Rebecca loved the flickering Hanukkah lights that seemed to melt away the winter darkness, if only for a week.

Mama came into the kitchen lugging a bag of potatoes. "I think that's finally enough!" she declared, pouring the potatoes into a wooden bin near the doorway.

Rebecca started to tell her about the centerpiece. Mama would know if it was the right thing to do. "Today in school we started a project," she began. "Do you think it's all right if—"

"Oy, such a load!" exclaimed Bubbie, Rebecca's grandmother. She set a bulging oilcloth bag filled

13

with potatoes on the work shelf of the tall kitchen cabinet.

Rebecca decided to wait and talk to Mama after Bubbie went upstairs to her own apartment. She didn't want to mention the centerpiece in front of Bubbie until she knew whether Mama would approve. Instead, Rebecca bundled into her coat and scarf.

"I'm going out to feed the pigeons for Mr. Rossi," she announced. "He's got a bad cold." Then she remembered the lost cat. "Have you seen Pasta around? Mr. Rossi thinks she's lost."

"That messy cat," Bubbie said. "Always under my feet on the stairs. Good riddance!"

Rebecca dashed out the front door of the building and down the steps. She knocked lightly at Mr. Rossi's door, which had its own entrance. When there was no answer, she rapped harder. After what seemed like forever, he opened the door a crack.

"I think you not coming. Kids today is so lazy. Here," he said, handing Rebecca two small pails. "Fill one dish in every cage with water, one with seeds." Then he handed her a damp rag. "You gotta clean out the dishes first." Rebecca tried to smile at him, but Mr. Rossi had already shut the door. He didn't like children, Rebecca knew. He especially didn't seem to like her.

The birds cooed and flapped in their cages when Rebecca approached, as if they knew it was time to eat. One pair of birds lived in each cage. Mr. Rossi had built a slanted roof over the cages for the winter. Rebecca thought the pigeons looked nice and cozy in their sheltered home.

She looked out at the rooftops that stretched across the neighborhood as far as she could see. None of them had pigeon cages. The gentle birds living on her rooftop made Rebecca feel that there wasn't another building in New York that was as special as hers.

She opened each cage, cleaned and filled the seed and water dishes, and made sure the latches were secure. The pigeons dipped their beaks into the water dishes and pecked eagerly at the seeds. As Rebecca watched them, a large white pigeon sailed onto the roof above the cages.

"Where did you come from?" Rebecca asked softly. She put a few seeds into her hand, and the bird pecked at them. "Oh, you're hungry, are you?"

15

Rebecca giggled as its beak tickled her palm.

Was this a wild bird that had come for a handout, or had one of Mr. Rossi's birds escaped? She had noticed that one cage was empty. Rebecca placed a small pile of seeds at the bird's feet and hurried down the stairs.

As she passed the door that led to the basement, she heard a strange mewling sound. The door was open, and the steep wooden stairs were dark. Rebecca stopped and heard the faint sound again. Maybe Pasta had chased after a mouse and had gotten hurt. She stepped down the rickety stairway and tried to see in the dim light. Pieces of coal littered the floor, and dirty buckets were strewn about. Only Mr. Rossi came down here, when the furnace needed more coal.

Rebecca saw a slight movement against one wall. She could barely make out a heap of rags and a shadowy shape on top. Then she heard a soft mew. It was Pasta! Rebecca picked her way down the steps and inched closer. As she reached down to pick up the lost cat, Pasta hissed at her. Rebecca jumped back, but not before she saw two tiny kittens nuzzling their mother for milk. Pasta's eyes were wide, but the kittens' eyes were shut tight.

"No wonder you don't want me to get too close," Rebecca said softly. "Don't worry, Pasta, I'll help you take good care of your babies."

"Mr. Rossi!" she called as she approached his apartment. She banged on the door.

"So, you have trouble already, eh?" the old man wheezed.

"Oh, no," Rebecca said. "No trouble at all. And I found Pasta. She's in the basement with two new kittens. They're so tiny! Wait till you see them."

"Work, work, work," Mr. Rossi complained. "And more mouths to feed!"

"There's other news, too. While I was feeding the birds, a big white pigeon landed on the roof, and I was afraid one of your birds had gotten loose."

Mr. Rossi's face brightened. "A white pigeon?" he asked. "Open the empty cage for it. But first take the message."

"Message?" Rebecca asked. "The bird can't talk!"

"Maybe not," he said mysteriously, "but it can bring news." He looked at Rebecca doubtfully. "You don't see a little tube on its leg? Inside is a note.

Open the tube and bring the message to me, yes?"

Rebecca bounded up the stairs, nearly crashing into Bubbie as her grandmother headed upstairs.

"What?" Bubbie exclaimed, moving out of the way. "This is a race you're in?"

But Rebecca just yelled, "Sorry! I have to catch a bird!" She opened the creaky roof door slowly, so that she wouldn't frighten the new pigeon away. It was still standing on the rooftop, cocking its head in her direction. Rebecca approached cautiously, but it didn't seem to mind when she picked it up and pried open the slender tube that was attached to its leg.

"Oh, you *do* have a secret message!" she cried, gently removing a thin, tightly rolled paper. She wanted to know what it said, but that would be like reading Mr. Rossi's mail. After all, it wasn't a message for her. She pocketed the rolled note and opened the door of the empty cage. Without any coaxing, the white pigeon fluttered in.

Questions flooded into Rebecca's mind as she filled the bird's dishes. Where had the white pigeon come from? How had it found her building? And what did the message say?

Rebecca was sure Mr. Rossi had the answers, but

he might think she was being nosy and get angry with her if she asked. She hurried back down the steps to his apartment. When Mr. Rossi opened his door, Rebecca hesitated, gathering her courage. Just as she handed him the thin paper and opened her mouth to speak, Mr. Rossi pointed to a dish of milk. "Now you gotta feed Pasta, too." Then he started coughing. He waved Rebecca away and closed the door with a firm *click*.

A SECRET SHARED

Rebecca couldn't wait to tell her sisters about the kittens and the mysterious white pigeon, but when she headed to the bedroom, there was a sign on the closed door: *"Keep Out!"*

"Let me in," Rebecca demanded, giving the door a kick. "This is my room, too!"

Sadie came to the door and opened it no wider than Mr. Rossi had opened his. "You can come in, I guess," she whispered. "But be quiet!"

Sophie was sitting on her bed, hiding something behind her back.

"What are you doing?" Rebecca asked. Her sisters looked at each other.

"Go ahead and tell her," Sophie said.

But Sadie hesitated. "Can you keep a secret?"

"Of course I can," Rebecca said.

"Do you absolutely, positively promise not to breathe a word of what we're doing?" Sadie demanded.

Rebecca plunked herself down on her sisters' bed and crossed her arms across her chest. "I don't care if you tell me or not! I have secrets of my own."

Sophie carefully pulled out a long table scarf embroidered with gay flowers. "I'm sewing this for Bubbie," she whispered. "We've been making Hanukkah gifts to surprise everyone."

"You made something for everyone?" Rebecca asked, impressed.

"Well, not yet," said Sadie.

Sophie added, "We're running out of time."

Rebecca picked up one end of the table scarf. "Bubbie will love this. She can put it in her parlor. Do you have something for Grandpa?"

Sadie shook her head, and the tight curl at her forehead bobbed. "We're stumped on what to make for him," she admitted. "Any ideas?"

Rebecca thought for a moment. Grandpa wore a prayer cap on his head all the time, even under his hat when he went out. "He might like a new *yarmulke*," she suggested. Then her face lit up. "Maybe I could crochet one for him. I have some silvery gray thread."

"It would match his hair," Sadie quipped. The three girls giggled together.

"All right," Sadie decided. "You can help. Just remember—it's our secret! Now, what's yours?"

Rebecca sat up straighter, delighted that her sisters were including her in their holiday plan. For once, they weren't treating her like a baby. She pulled out her crochet bag and chose a hook. "Guess what? Pasta had kittens! They're in the basement, and their eyes are still shut. They must have just been born. I got to bring Pasta a dish of milk."

"I can't wait to see them," Sadie said. "They're like a Christmas present for Mr. Rossi."

Rebecca laughed. "I don't think he's too happy about having more cats, but he was excited about something else. He got a secret message today," she announced with an air of importance. "It came by *pigeon!*"

"Really?" Sophie asked, her eyebrows lifting in surprise. "I didn't know Mr. Rossi's birds were homing pigeons. I read in my history book that when Napoleon lost the battle of Waterloo, a carrier pigeon brought the news to France four days faster than a soldier on horseback."

"Maybe the message is about the war in Europe," Sadie exclaimed. "What did it say?"

"I don't know yet," Rebecca said, looping stitches with the crochet hook. "After all, it was a secret. I'm going to try to get Mr. Rossi to tell me tomorrow."

But she wasn't sure how. *What would Rebecca of Sunnybrook Farm do?* She was pretty sure *that* Rebecca wouldn't lose her courage at the last moment. *Maybe if I just ask him, he'll tell me everything!* But Mr. Rossi would have to open his door more than a crack.

A knock sounded on the bedroom door, and the girls froze. "Don't come in!" they squealed.

"Supper!" Mama called. "Whatever you three are up to, it's going to have to wait."

Rebecca started singing as she walked into the kitchen. "Jingle bells, jingle bells, jingle all the way . . ." She had just reached the part about dashing through the snow when Bubbie swooped into the kitchen.

"What you are singing?" she demanded.

Rebecca stopped in mid-verse. "It's a song we sing in school," she said. Why was Bubbie upset?

"This song is for Christmas, not for you!" Bubbie chided her.

"But it's just about riding through snow on a sleigh," Rebecca protested. "You told me you loved sleigh rides when you were a girl in Russia."

"Never mind about Russia!" Bubbie said sternly. "No more of this Christmas singing."

Mama pulled a steaming noodle casserole from the oven. The kitchen filled with the scent of cheese and a hint of cinnamon.

"Christmas is all around us, I'm afraid," said Mama. "It seems there are more decorations in the city every year."

"It's all over the neighborhood yet!" Bubbie complained, cutting big squares of the noodle *kugel.* "The shop windows have little trees with colored balls hanging, and everywhere are these round things—reefs!" She made a big circle with her hand, and sputtered, "Can you believe it? There's even

one hanging from the bagel man's cart on Orchard Street!"

"Ahh," Mama nodded as they all sat down at the table. *"Wreaths. That lovely greenery, and the pretty bows."*

In her excitement about the kittens and the white pigeon, Rebecca had nearly forgotten about her school project. If Bubbie didn't want her to sing "Jingle Bells," she would surely be angry if she found out Rebecca was making a centerpiece with greenery and a red bow! But Mama had said the wreaths were lovely. Maybe *she* would like the decoration.

Benny waited as Papa cut a square of kugel into bite-sized pieces for him. "Papa, did you hang a reef at the shoe store?"

Papa fidgeted with his tie. "No, not a wreath," he said slowly.

"Then *what?*" Benny insisted. He speared a noodle with his fork.

"Well, just a few green boughs." Papa looked sheepishly at Bubbie, who was frowning. "We have to make the window look festive," he explained, "like the other stores."

Maybe Papa could put my centerpiece in the store,

25

Rebecca thought. But as she looked at Bubbie's scowling face, she felt sure her grandmother wouldn't approve.

Rebecca looked around the table uncertainly. "Miss Maloney says Christmas is an American holiday—for everyone to celebrate," she said.

"*Fooey!*" Grandpa declared, slicing a loaf of thick black bread. "Christmas is a Christian holiday. We are Jewish, so we don't celebrate it, no matter how American we are."

Rebecca was silent. If Grandpa learned of the school project, he would be as upset as Bubbie.

"Our friends at school say Hanukkah isn't a very important holiday for Jews, but Christmas is the most important holiday for Christians," Sadie put in. "The students who celebrate Christmas get gifts, and some of our Jewish friends do, too!"

"We already have the very best gift of all," Papa said firmly. "In America we have the gift of being free to celebrate our own holiday."

No one else said a word, but Rebecca and her sisters exchanged knowing looks. Every year, Grandpa gave each of the children a shiny half-dollar. The money was called Hanukkah *gelt* in

Yiddish, and it carried on an old tradition. Rebecca loved the feel of the heavy silver coin, and the money would last her for a long time. But when it came to presents, this year was going to be different. Everyone would receive a gift, not just the children. Wouldn't Papa be surprised!

After the dishes were cleared away, the twins went off to their room together, but now Rebecca didn't mind. She knew they weren't leaving her out. She would work on Grandpa's yarmulke before she went to bed. How exciting it was to share a secret with her sisters!

Victor settled at the kitchen table to do his homework, complaining about how many arithmetic problems he had to work out.

"Here is a problem for you to figure," Grandpa said with a sparkle in his eyes. "There are eight nights of Hanukkah, and we light one additional candle each night. Every night the candles burn all the way down, and the next night we start with new ones. So, how many candles do we need to last the whole week?" Victor's eyes narrowed with concentration. "I give a little hint," Grandpa added. "Don't forget to count the extra shammas each night!"

As Victor started writing down a long column of numbers, Rebecca leaned toward Grandpa and whispered, "Forty-four!" It was just loud enough for her brother to hear.

Victor glared at her. "You already knew the answer!" he accused her. "No one could figure it out that fast."

"I can," Rebecca declared. "I'm used to Miss Maloney's Arithmetic Teasers. We figure out problems in our head in no time." She went into the parlor and pulled a chair closer to the fireplace so that she'd be warm while she read her library book.

"Such a fine mathematics student you are," Grandpa said, pulling up a chair beside her. "There is a word I hear for this . . ." He thought for a moment, trying to remember. "Whiz!" he grinned. "You are arithmetic whiz!"

"Then let her do my homework!" Victor called from the kitchen.

Mama switched on the parlor lamp. A soft glow fell across Rebecca's book.

Grandpa opened his Yiddish newspaper. "So, what your book is about?"

"It's the best book," Rebecca said, "but

there are some parts that I don't quite understand. Listen to this." She read aloud to Grandpa. "'The traits of unknown forebears had been wrought into her fibre.' What do you suppose that means?"

Grandpa rubbed his beard. "Maybe if it was in Yiddish, I could help you."

Rebecca looked down at the book and then back at Grandpa. "Mostly, the story is about a poor girl named Rebecca who is sent to live with two aunts she barely knows, just so she can go to school," Rebecca said. She couldn't imagine having to leave her family and live with strangers. "Rebecca's so brave. I don't think I could ever do that."

Grandpa patted her hand. "Courage comes when you need it," he said, speaking in Yiddish, as he often did. "I didn't think I could leave Russia and come to America. It was hard, starting all over again and not speaking one word of English!"

"That took real courage," Rebecca agreed. Her cousin Ana had done that, and Rose, too. Maybe that was why Rose had been brave enough to tell Miss Maloney she didn't want to make the center- piece. Standing up to a teacher wasn't nearly as hard as moving to a new country. Still, Rebecca knew she didn't even have the nerve to question Miss Maloney about the assignment.

She looked over at Grandpa as he read his newspaper. "Miss Maloney thinks Christmas is so important that we should all put up decorations to celebrate," Rebecca said quietly.

Grandpa shook his head and made a *tsk-tsk* sound with his tongue. Rebecca felt a flutter of guilt. It was as if Grandpa had declared, "You must not make the centerpiece!"

Rebecca glanced toward the family's menorah gleaming on the windowsill. The tinted candles stood tall, waiting for the first night of Hanukkah. "Grandpa, is it true that Hanukkah isn't really a very important Jewish holiday?" she asked.

Grandpa folded his newspaper onto his lap. "Long ago," he began, "the Jews were ruled by a king who prayed to statues of different gods. The king decreed that all his subjects must worship as he did. His soldiers rampaged through the temple where the Jews prayed and smashed everything they could. It was a frightening time. Many Jews were afraid to disobey the king's law. Others just wanted to fit in, to be like everyone else."

"Grandpa, is it true that Hanukkah isn't really
a very important Jewish holiday?" Rebecca asked.

"Miss Maloney thinks everyone should dress and speak the same," Rebecca said. "And especially, no talking in Yiddish!"

"Immigrants have to learn new ways to live here in America," Grandpa admitted. "But we can't forget who we are, even if it means being a little different."

Rebecca felt a wave of understanding. "Wait a minute—that's what the sentence in my book is about!" she exclaimed.

Grandpa looked puzzled, and now it was Rebecca's turn to explain. "When it says that 'the traits of unknown forebears were wrought into her fibre,' I think it's just a fancy way of saying that the habits that made Rebecca different from other people were passed down from her ancestors. That makes her special. Do you think the Jews felt like that, long ago?"

"Absolutely!" Grandpa said. "Many of them refused to give up their religion, even for the king. One brave group fought the king's entire army—and they won. If they hadn't, there wouldn't be any Jews left today. That's part of what we celebrate every year on Hanukkah." Grandpa reached over and

*"Grandpa, is it true that Hanukkah isn't really
a very important Jewish holiday?" Rebecca asked.*

31

"Miss Maloney thinks everyone should dress and speak the same," Rebecca said. "And especially, no talking in Yiddish!"

"Immigrants have to learn new ways to live here in America," Grandpa admitted. "But we can't forget who we are, even if it means being a little different."

Rebecca felt a wave of understanding. "Wait a minute—that's what the sentence in my book is about!" she exclaimed.

Grandpa looked puzzled, and now it was Rebecca's turn to explain. "When it says that 'the traits of unknown forebears were wrought into her fibre,' I think it's just a fancy way of saying that the habits that made Rebecca different from other people were passed down from her ancestors. That makes her special. Do you think the Jews felt like that, long ago?"

"Absolutely!" Grandpa said. "Many of them refused to give up their religion, even for the king. One brave group fought the king's entire army—and they won. If they hadn't, there wouldn't be any Jews left today. That's part of what we celebrate every year on Hanukkah." Grandpa reached over and tapped Rebecca on her head. "Do you think that's important?" Rebecca nodded solemnly.

Grandpa pointed to the menorah. "Remember why we light the candles for eight nights?" He didn't wait for Rebecca to answer. "When the Jews cleaned their temple, they wanted to re-light the special lamp that stood near the altar. But they could find just one small vial of sacred oil to place in the lamp. It was only enough to last for one day, but that little bit of oil burned for eight full days. Many thought it was a miracle, to show them they had done the right thing in fighting against the king."

"In my book, Rebecca Randall always does what she thinks is right," Rebecca told Grandpa, "even if grown-ups sometimes get angry."

"A girl with *chutzpah*," Grandpa said.

Rebecca thought about the school project again. Maybe she needed a little chutzpah, too. Maybe she should be brave enough to tell Miss Maloney she wouldn't make the centerpiece.

As Grandpa adjusted his prayer cap, Rebecca remembered she still needed to work on his present. She stood up and faked a yawn. "Well, I'm going off to bed," she fibbed.

Bubbie looked up from her crocheting. "What, so early?" she asked. "You hardly read two pages! You feel sick, maybe?"

"No, I'm just really tired," Rebecca pretended, and slipped into her room. The twins were busily working. Rebecca could hardly believe they were letting her be part of their plan. It was as though she had just tasted something new and delicious. For now, she could forget her worries about school and the centerpiece and simply enjoy sharing a secret with her sisters. Round and round she crocheted the prayer cap for Grandpa, until it grew big enough to fit on his head. She finished it off with two white stripes around the edge and held it up proudly.

Sadie patted her shoulder. "You actually made a yarmulke!" she said. "It's beautiful. How about another one for Papa?"

Rebecca nodded with enthusiasm. This year, when her parents gave out Hanukkah gelt, she and her sisters would have something to give them in return.

"This is going to be the best Hanukkah ever," Rebecca whispered as she reached for a new ball of thread.

MINDING
MISS MALONEY

"I can't wait to wear my holiday dress,"
Rebecca said the next morning. "It's almost
spandy new."

Mama blinked in surprise. "I suppose that's
Rebecca of Sunnybrook Farm talking again," she
laughed. "Ever since you started reading that book,
I feel as if I have four daughters instead of three!"
She put a plate of breakfast rolls on the table. "Your
dress may be spandy new, but you are a lot taller
than you were a few months ago. I'm sure the sleeves
and the hem need to be let down a few inches. I have
so much cooking to do, I'll never have a chance to
sew it before tomorrow night, when Hanukkah
begins. You'll just have to wear a school dress."

Rebecca's heart sank. "But Mama," she argued, "with company coming I wanted to wear my holiday dress!"

The twins came in for breakfast. "You should have thought of that before you grew," Sadie teased. "Did you think your dress would grow along with you?" Sophie smiled at the joke. As they sat down, there was a musical tinkling sound.

"I hear bells!" Benny cried in astonishment. He tilted his head back to look up at Sadie and Sophie. "It's you!" he laughed, pleased that he had solved the mystery.

 The twins had tied long red ribbons in their hair, and a small metal bell dangled at the end of each streamer. Every time they moved, the bells gave a merry jingle. Benny reached up, trying to shake them.

Mama's lips pursed into a thin line. "You can take those ribbons off right now," she said.

"But Mama, they're just for fun!" Sadie protested.

"All the girls are wearing them," Sophie added.

"Well, I know two girls who are not," Mama said firmly. "You're going to school to study, not to be in a costume play!" She held out her hand with the palm up, waiting.

"Oh, Mama," the twins whined.

"You will not leave the house with such silliness," Mama said. "I can just imagine what Bubbie would say if she saw you!"

With a pout, the twins untied the ribbons and handed them over. As Rebecca brushed past her sisters to get her coat, she leaned toward them and hummed a few bars of "Jingle Bells" so softly that only they heard. Their faces flushed with anger. Giggling, Rebecca grabbed her coat and ducked out the door before they could catch her.

On the way out, Rebecca stopped to visit the new kittens. They were sleeping soundly, and Pasta watched them protectively. Rebecca didn't try to touch them—not yet. There would be plenty of time to play with them when they grew bigger.

Rose was waiting outside for Rebecca. "I like the lions carved on each side of your row house door," Rose said as the girls fell into step together. "Otherwise, your building looks like every other one on the street."

It was true. Each brick row house had a

tall front stoop, four floors, and large windows spaced evenly apart. "On the outside, the buildings do look pretty much the same," Rebecca agreed, "but my building is different in another way, too."

"What's different about it besides the lions?" Rose asked.

"Pigeons!" Rebecca exclaimed as they turned the corner. "Mr. Rossi, our janitor, keeps pigeons on the roof. He uses them to send messages!"

"They must be homing pigeons," Rose said, her eyes wide. "What are the messages about?"

"I tried to ask him yesterday, after I fed the birds," Rebecca said, "but he's so grumpy. Before I could say a word, he shut his door right in my face! He doesn't like anyone—especially kids. He's always complaining when we play in front of the building." She waved her hand, as if dismissing Mr. Rossi. "Well, I don't like *him* very much, either— just his pigeons. And now his cat has kittens. So I guess I should feel lucky he lives in our building." The two girls hurried on to school, their arms linked together.

When class began that morning, Miss Maloney was in a festive mood. Instead of singing "The Star-

Spangled Banner" to start the day, she had the class
sing one of the carols they had learned. Everyone
stood and sang "Hark! The Herald Angels Sing."
Rebecca loved singing, and the melody was
beautiful, but as she came to the last lines, she fell
silent. "With the angelic host proclaim, Christ is
born in Bethlehem," sang the other students.
Rebecca wasn't sure what an angelic host was, but
she *was* sure that if Bubbie had scolded her for
singing "Jingle Bells," she would be furious if she
found out Rebecca was singing this.

"As my Christmas present to each of you,"
Miss Maloney said when they finished, "there will
be no penmanship exercises and no arithmetic
lesson today." The class erupted in cheers. "Instead,
we will spend the entire morning working on our
centerpieces."

The students crowded to the back of the room,
where their unfinished decorations were lined up.
Rebecca found hers without even checking for her
name on the bottom. It was the one with the candle
set to the side and the greenery piled extra high. She
held it one way, and then turned it another. In spite
of her misgivings, she couldn't help admiring the

effect. After all, it was just a decoration. How could making something so pretty be wrong? She would try not to think about what to do with it until she was done.

"Work quickly, children," Miss Maloney said. "The glue must be dry by tomorrow so that you can take your projects home."

Tomorrow! Rebecca hadn't known she would have to take her project home so soon! She remembered Mama's displeasure with the twins for wearing red ribbons and bells. And Bubbie didn't like to hear or see anything that smacked of Christmas. Rebecca swallowed hard, and a taste like sour lemons washed down her throat. She couldn't take a Christmas decoration home, no matter how pretty it was.

Miss Maloney had said there were no extra candles. *If my candle broke, I wouldn't be able to finish my decoration,* she thought. The bright red candle seemed like a lighthouse ready to shine its beacon across a sea of greens. It would be wasteful to spoil it, but she saw no other way to get out of the project. Taking a deep breath, she turned the centerpiece upside down and gave it a shake. A few pine needles dropped from the rustling branches, but the candle didn't budge. Rebecca had glued it down firmly. She let out a deep sigh and turned it right side up again.

"Mother is going to love my decoration," Gertie declared. "She's already put balsam around the windows. I think she'll want this on the mantel, over the tinsel cord."

"You put up Christmas decorations?" Rebecca asked. "But you're Jewish!"

"We don't *celebrate* Christmas," said Gertie. "We just like the decorations. As Miss Maloney says, it's an American holiday."

Rebecca had heard that some Jewish families had Christmas decorations, but she had never actually known anyone who did. Her family would never agree with Gertie's, she was certain. She set her unfinished centerpiece on her desk and poked at the spiky pine branches.

"Isn't it fun making this centerpiece?" Lucy grinned. "It's so much better than practicing handwriting!"

"That's true," Rebecca agreed. "But then, your family celebrates Christmas, so they'll enjoy the

41

decoration." Very softly she added, "I don't know what I'm going to do with mine." She followed Lucy to Miss Maloney's desk and gathered up handfuls of berries and pinecones.

"Aren't you going to give it to your mother?" Lucy asked with surprise.

Rebecca shook her head. The centerpiece could never be a Hanukkah gift. "We don't have decorations," she explained. "We celebrate a different holiday called Hanukkah."

"Then you don't even have a Christmas tree?" Lucy asked.

Rebecca shook her head. "Nope."

Lucy put her arm around Rebecca. "That's too bad," she said.

"No, it isn't," Rebecca said. "Our whole family is getting together and we're going to have a real feast. Every night we sing songs and play a game called *dreidel*."

Lucy looked puzzled. "On Christmas, we celebrate the birth of baby Jesus," she said. "We put up beautiful decorations to make everything sparkle, even in the middle of winter. What does Hanukkah celebrate?"

Rebecca remembered what Grandpa had told her. "Hanukkah is also called the Festival of Lights, because we light special candles every night. That's to remember how Jewish people long ago fought a king's army so that they could worship in their own temple." Rebecca's excitement about Hanukkah bubbled out of her. "It's my absolute favorite holiday of all, and it lasts a whole week!"

"But there's nothing wrong with you making this centerpiece, is there?" Lucy asked.

"I don't know," Rebecca admitted.

Miss Maloney's pinched voice caught Rebecca's ear, and she turned away from Lucy. "Oh, dear me," Miss Maloney was saying to Rose. "You don't want all your pinecones jumbled in one place!" Rebecca watched Miss Maloney snap off several of the tiny pinecones. "You must balance the decorations around the entire centerpiece," she instructed. Globs of white glue stuck to the branches where Miss Maloney had removed pinecones, and Rose's candle tilted crookedly.

"I don't care what it looks like," Rose muttered to Rebecca under her breath.

Back at her desk, Rebecca began nestling berries

and pinecones together on the pine boughs. Each time she bent over the fragrant greenery, she imagined she was deep in a pine forest. She stepped back and looked at what she had accomplished so far. It was such a beautiful decoration. If only it weren't for Christmas!

Miss Maloney stopped at Rebecca's desk. "How lovely!" she exclaimed. "Rebecca, I believe you have an artistic flair!" She held the centerpiece up. "Look, everyone," she said, "this design is a bit different. The greenery is so full, and the pinecones and berries are placed together beautifully. Good job."

Rebecca thought this should be another moment of unbounded joy. Miss Maloney had praised her work out of all the projects in the class. If only it had been a page of perfect arithmetic problems, instead of this!

❧

"What are you going to do with your centerpiece tomorrow?" Rebecca asked Rose as they walked home. The air was so cold that it seemed as if her words froze as she spoke.

Rose didn't hesitate. "Throw it away."

"How could you throw away something so

"What are you going to do with your centerpiece tomorrow?"
Rebecca asked Rose as they walked home.

pretty?" Rebecca asked. "And it has a spandy new candle in it, too!"

Rose could barely shrug through her heavy coat and scarf, but Rebecca saw the familiar gesture. "Miss Maloney says to make it, so I do. My mother won't have Christmas decorations in the house, so I'll toss it in the trash before she ever sees it. What are you going to do with yours?"

Rebecca copied Rose's shrug, but she didn't have an answer. How could she give Grandpa a prayer cap and at the same time bring home a Christmas decoration? Grandpa would be so disappointed in her after all he had explained about the importance of Hanukkah. Maybe she would have to throw her centerpiece away, too.

When Rebecca got home, she tried to stop thinking about the decoration. She no longer wanted to talk to Mama about the school project.

"Are you going to feed the pigeons again?" Mama asked. Rebecca nodded. Caring for the pigeons would help take her mind off the center-piece. Perhaps today she would find out about the mysterious message that had arrived on the white pigeon.

"I've got some chicken soup for Mr. Rossi," Mama said. "It will help his cold. You can take it down when you go to get the bird food."

Mr. Rossi was still his cranky self when he answered his door. "Don't let in the cold air," he scolded, barely opening the door a crack. He had tied a wool scarf around his neck and tucked it into his bathrobe. He quickly took the jar of warm soup and handed out the seed and water pails. "Don't forget to bring me cat's dish, too. She's gonna need lotsa milk."

Rebecca spoke up quickly, before he turned away. "Excuse me," she began. "What message did the white—"

But the old man loudly cleared his throat with a gurgling sound. "Your mama is a nice lady," he said gruffly through the narrow opening. He hesitated as if he was reluctant to say anything pleasant and then added "*Grazie*" as he firmly shut the door.

Rebecca climbed the stairs to the roof. The pairs of pigeons in each cage nestled close to each other for warmth. Some had tucked their heads under their wings, content in their sheltered nook. The white pigeon stood alone on its perch.

What was the secret message Mr. Rossi had received? Maybe Sadie was right that it was about the war in Europe. Only last week, Rebecca had heard Papa worrying out loud that America might end up in the war, too. Could Mr. Rossi be training carrier pigeons for the United States Army? She caught her breath. Imagine such extraordinary goings-on, right here in an ordinary row house!

Rebecca thought about this as she fed the cooing pigeons. If only people could appreciate how her row house was different from all the rest. In her book, Rebecca Randall said it made a big difference what you called things. Instead of plain old Randall Farm, Rebecca called her home Sunnybrook Farm so that people who heard the name would picture the sparkling brook and the sunlit fields. No one would guess her farmhouse looked like any other.

Perhaps I should give my home a name, too, Rebecca mused. She looked at the birds and concentrated. She wanted a name that painted a picture of the cozy pigeon roost—and also hinted of hidden secrets.

"I know!" she said out loud. "Pigeon Cove. From now on, I live at Pigeon Cove."

A PERFECT
PRESENT

At school on Friday, Rebecca's class
helped to decorate the auditorium. The
boys climbed on chairs and hung paper
snowflakes in the large windows. Rebecca helped
the girls drape paper chains made with red and
green links along the edge of the stage. A glittering
Christmas tree decorated with candles and thin
peppermint sticks stood next to the American flag.
But Rebecca didn't feel part of the excitement. She
was too worried about what to do with the centerpiece she had made. Today was the day she had to
take it home.

Back in the classroom, Rebecca's eyes were
constantly drawn to the collection of festive

centerpieces that covered a huge table against the wall. Each time she looked behind her, the decorations seemed to take up more space, growing like magic evergreens in her imagination.

"As soon as you've put on your coats and hats, you may pick up your decorations," Miss Maloney told the students at the end of the day. "Carry them carefully on your way home."

The room seemed to swirl around Rebecca in a dizzying kaleidoscope of colors as students hurried from the coat closet to the table, pulling on thick woolen mittens and tugging at their trailing scarves. The festive centerpieces were carried out in a parade of ribbons and greenery.

Rebecca's throat felt tight and dry as she lingered at the table. Her centerpiece sat alone, looking abandoned. What should she do with it?

"I hope your family enjoys the gift you made," Miss Maloney said, smiling.

"Thank you," Rebecca said politely, but she was sure the only gifts her family would enjoy were the ones she had made with her sisters.

The sharp air stung Rebecca's cheeks as she stepped outside. Ahead of her, she caught a glimpse of Rose, Gertie, and Lucy as they disappeared across the park. Rebecca trudged home the long way around. She needed time to think. She had to decide what to do with her decoration before she got back to Pigeon Cove.

As Rebecca passed a row of stores with small heaps of trash piled next to the curb, a flash of red caught her eye. A centerpiece leaned against a stack of old newspapers. There were globs of white glue on some of the branches, and a red candle tilted to one side. It was Rose's decoration. Rebecca couldn't bear to see it tossed out with the trash. She hated the thought of throwing away her own centerpiece. But what choice did she have?

Big flakes of snow began to fall from the thick gray sky. She hurried across the street, dodging a delivery wagon. The horse was draped in a red blanket, and his ears stuck up through slits on each side of a floppy green hat. "Merry Christmas!" called the man driving the wagon. Rebecca gave him a half-hearted wave.

Just before she turned onto her street, she stopped next to a pile of empty wooden crates.

Wisps of packing straw littered the sidewalk and blew against the lamppost. Rebecca set her centerpiece down on a broken crate and took one final look at what she had made. The red candle rose above the fresh greens, and she could almost picture a small flame flickering at the top. Just as she bent over to breathe in the woodsy fragrance for the last time, a man came storming out of a shop behind her.

"Get away," he shouted. "Leave that stuff alone!"

Rebecca grabbed her centerpiece and hurried off. The shopkeeper must have thought she was picking through his trash—but she had only been leaving something behind.

The snowflakes fell steadily, and by the time Rebecca arrived at her apartment, they had blanketed the sidewalk and covered everything with a layer of white. Rebecca shook off her scarf and unbuttoned her coat before climbing the steps to her apartment. Her stomach fluttered. *Please let Mama be there*, she wished, *and not Bubbie.* She hoped Mama would understand why she had made the decoration and not get angry. She took a deep, raggedy breath and trudged up the stairs.

The mouthwatering smell of frying potato pancakes filled the hallway. Mama was home! Rebecca pushed open the door, but instead of her mother standing at the stove, it was Bubbie who was dropping spoonfuls of lumpy potato batter into the sizzling frying pan. Quickly, Rebecca hid the centerpiece under her coat.

"Happy Hanukkah," Bubbie cried, lifting a browned potato pancake from the pan and adding it to a pile on a platter. "Come have a little taste. You can *nosh* on a hot latke before everybody comes."

Benny was spinning a dreidel across the table, next to the vegetable grater. Peeled potatoes were heaped in a bowl beside it. "I'm going to win all the candies tonight when we play dreidel," Benny said.

"Where's Mama?" Rebecca gulped.

"Upstairs in my kitchen, having a nice quiet bath," Bubbie replied. "Come, take off your coat, nosh a little, and then grate some more potatoes for me."

Rebecca couldn't take off her coat or Bubbie would see what she was hiding. She picked up a potato and tried to grate it with one hand while she held on to the centerpiece with her other hand. The heat in the kitchen felt suffocating.

"What you are doing?" Bubbie scolded. "Take off coat and wash hands first."

"I see a secret!" Benny announced. He started dancing around Rebecca, pointing to the bulge under her coat. "What are you hiding? Is it a surprise?"

Bubbie turned away from the sizzling oil and wiped her hands on her apron. Rebecca felt as if the oil was boiling inside her, sputtering and crackling. She swallowed hard, pushing back the lump in her throat, and pulled out the Christmas decoration.

"I'm s-sorry, Bubbie!" she stammered, tears welling in her eyes. "It was a school project."

Bubbie took the centerpiece from Rebecca and turned it around in her hands. Rebecca couldn't meet her grandmother's eyes. Her head hung down and she rubbed her shoe against a rough nick in the linoleum floor. The only sound she heard was the sizzling of latkes in the frying pan. Bubbie was silent.

Slowly, Rebecca lifted her eyes. But instead of the angry frown she expected, Bubbie's eyes were crinkled at the corners, and she was smiling.

"What's to be sorry?" she said, pinching Rebecca's cheek. "It's a beautiful thing you made." She set it on the table as Benny leaned in for a closer look. The twins came in, dressed in matching wool skirts with crisp white shirtwaists. Bubbie motioned them over. "Come give a look!" she said.

"Oooh," crooned Sophie, "it's so pretty. Did you make it, Beckie?" Rebecca nodded cautiously.

"I love it," Sadie said. "Especially the little berries." She brushed them lightly with her fingertips.

"I was going to throw it away on my way home from school," Rebecca blurted out, "but I just couldn't." Bubbie and everything around her blurred as tears spilled down Rebecca's hot cheeks. "I didn't know what to do. Miss Maloney said all Americans celebrate Christmas."

Bubbie put her hands on Rebecca's shoulders and looked into her eyes. "Teacher is right, and she is wrong," Bubbie said. "Some Americans celebrate Christmas, and some don't. But at school, you must do what teacher tells you." She turned to the center-piece again. "Now, such a piece of work! What shall we do with it?"

Rebecca wiped her eyes. "I don't want it, Bubbie. Let's just throw it away."

"Oh, that would be awful," Sadie said. "Let's leave it for now, and decide later." Sophie nodded.

Bubbie clapped her hands together. "So, finish grating potatoes, then feed pigeons, then wash up and put on clean dress before everyone comes." She turned back to the latkes, flipping them to brown on the other side.

"We'll take care of the potatoes, Beckie," Sadie offered. "You'll need time to get changed."

"Why bother," Rebecca mumbled. "Who wants to wear a boring old school dress on Hanukkah?"

Bubbie handed Rebecca a jar of vegetable soup. "Is for your Mr. Rossi, his cold should get better."

Rebecca hugged Bubbie tightly. "I thought you would be so angry with me," she whispered.

"For doing a good job with your schoolwork? Never!" Bubbie kissed Rebecca's forehead gently.

Rebecca took the jar of soup and walked slowly down the stairs to Mr. Rossi's door. His window was dark, and she could barely see a faint light coming from the back. She knocked,

56

"For doing a good job with your schoolwork? Never!" said Bubbie.

shivering as snowflakes blew against her face.

Mr. Rossi opened the door just a little wider than usual, grabbed Rebecca's sleeve, and pulled her in. "Quick! Close the door!" he ordered, rubbing his hands together. "It's so cold, and now snow!"

Rebecca shifted from one foot to the other, surprised to find herself inside Mr. Rossi's apartment instead of peering through a crack in the doorway. She wrinkled her nose at an awful smell that filled the air. Something on the stove was steaming and giving off a sour stink. What a difference from the tempting aroma of Bubbie's latkes! She quickly handed Mr. Rossi the soup and edged back to the door.

"I'm feeling better since your Mama sends me soup," he said. He pointed to the steaming pot. "The vinegar and salt is helping, too."

Rebecca cringed. "You're drinking vinegar and salt?" *No wonder Mr. Rossi is as sour as an old pickle,* she thought. *He drinks vinegar!*

"Oh, no," Mr. Rossi corrected her. "Not drink it. It's to gargle, for killing the germs."

While he shuffled off in his felt slippers to get the birdseed and a saucer of milk, Rebecca looked around the dim apartment, trying to breathe through her mouth and not her nose. Yellowed doilies were draped over the arms of a sagging couch, and a worn tablecloth covered a small kitchen table. The apartment felt strangely quiet, as if something was missing.

"Don't spill any," Mr. Rossi warned as he handed Rebecca the seed pails. "Even birdseed costs plenty." He reached for the doorknob.

If Mr. Rossi was getting better, then this might be her last chance to ask about the secret message. She fidgeted with the fringes on her scarf. She couldn't be shy now. "What was in the message?" she blurted out.

Mr. Rossi covered his mouth with a handkerchief as a new fit of coughing began. For a moment, Rebecca thought she would have to leave again without solving the mystery of the message. But finally Mr. Rossi cleared his throat and said hoarsely, "Is a note from my brother, Aldo, who lives in New Jersey." He swept his arm through the air, as if New Jersey were thousands of miles away instead of just across the Hudson River. "We both keep homing pigeons, just like we did back in Italy.

I keep a couple of his birds to send back to him with notes, and he keeps some of mine to fly to me. Pigeons go much faster than mail."

"Was it bad news?" she asked cautiously.

"Ah, no," Mr. Rossi said. "Aldo invites me to come spend Christmas with his family."

Rebecca had never thought about Mr. Rossi having any family at all. "I didn't know you had a brother," she said.

"I gotta big family, just like you. Some stay in Italy, but Aldo, he come to America with me. He gotta lot of children, all grown up, and they all bring their kids to Aldo's for Christmas." Mr. Rossi looked wistful. "I'd love to see the little ones, and Aldo's wife is a good cook. But since they moved to New Jersey, is so far away." Mr. Rossi sighed.

Rebecca would never have guessed that Mr. Rossi would want to spend Christmas with a roomful of children. "It really isn't that far away," she said. "You can take the ferry and be across the river in New Jersey in twenty minutes. Our cousin Max goes there every day to work for a movie company."

Mr. Rossi scratched the gray stubble on his chin

and seemed to consider this. "Twenty minutes, you say? If I am feeling better, and you would feed the pigeons and cat while I am gone," he said, almost to himself, "maybe . . ." For the first time, he looked directly at Rebecca, and she saw a glimmer of happiness in his eyes. "I write Aldo a note. Can you send it back?"

Rebecca felt a thrill of excitement. "I think I can." She was going to send a message by carrier pigeon! Even Rebecca of Sunnybrook Farm never got to do *that*. She waited in the dim apartment until Mr. Rossi handed her a tightly rolled slip of paper. It was so small, she could hardly believe that he had written a message inside. She tucked it into her pocket, took the pails, and headed back outside. Mr. Rossi shuffled behind her.

"Choose one of the gray pigeons," he said hoarsely. "They belong to Aldo, so they know the way." He cupped his hands together. "Hold the bird like this, carry to the edge of the roof, and toss it into the air," he said. "Be careful not to fall!"

"How does the pigeon know where to go?" Rebecca asked in amazement.

"Goes home, always home," Mr. Rossi said.

A snowy hush hung over the rooftop as Rebecca stepped to the cages. She fed one of the gray pigeons first, giving it extra seed. It would need a lot of strength to fly to New Jersey. When all the others were fed, she reached for the bird. Cupping it carefully in her hand, she felt its warmth and the rapid beating of its tiny heart. She tucked the paper message securely into the metal tube on its leg.

Rebecca carried the gray pigeon to the low wall that surrounded the roof. Below her, the East Side was blanketed with white. A few electric lights glowed faintly through apartment windows, and gaslights flickered in others. Soon, Rebecca knew, Jewish families would light the shammas and the first candle in their menorahs. The bright flames would welcome the first night of Hanukkah.

Rebecca held the pigeon close to her face and felt its warm feathers against her cold cheek. "Fly!" she whispered. "Fly home!" She opened her hands, and the bird rose gracefully into the sky.

Rebecca checked on the kittens, watching as they squirmed against their mother. Then she hurried back to her apartment, washed up, and went to change. Her holiday dress looked crisp and bright, but the sight of it filled her with disappointment. How could she have outgrown her best dress before she had worn it more than a few times? She lifted a starched but faded school dress from its hook.

"Aren't you going to wear your New Year's dress?" Sadie asked her.

"It's so pretty on you," Sophie added.

Rebecca felt her face flush. Since her sisters had let her help with the Hanukkah presents, she'd thought they had changed. Now she realized they were going to be as mean as ever. "You know Mama said it's too short," she snapped. "You don't have to make me feel worse."

"Mama could be wrong," Sadie said with a mischievous gleam in her eye. She pushed the dress at Rebecca. "You should try it on. Don't you agree, Sophie?"

"Definitely," her sister said. "I don't think you've grown much at all."

Rebecca fumed. *They still think I'm just a baby!* She wouldn't let them get away with teasing her like this. She tossed the dress onto her bed, but Sadie picked it up again.

"We'll help," Sophie said, pulling off the school dress Rebecca was wearing. Before Rebecca could fend them off, Sadie slipped the holiday dress over Rebecca's head.

"Take it off!" Rebecca protested. "It's too short."

"Not anymore," Sadie said.

Sophie grinned. "We fixed it for you!"

As the dress settled over her shoulders, Rebecca looked down. The cuffs reached the ends of her wrists, and the hem fell just above her knees. She was speechless.

"Happy Hanukkah!" Sadie and Sophie said together. "Did you think we wouldn't have a gift for you, too?"

Rebecca didn't know what to think. "It's perfect," she murmured.

"I sewed the left sleeve," Sadie said proudly.

"While I sewed the right," Sophie added. "We did the hem together and met in the middle!"

Rebecca looked down at the dress again and then up at her sisters. "Oh, thank you!" she said, throwing her arms around them both. "*Now* it feels like a holiday." Sophie tied the sash, and Sadie brushed Rebecca's hair to a shine and tied on a festive ribbon. Rebecca beamed.

"I'd better go return Mr. Rossi's pails before he thinks I fell off the roof!" she said.

"He's such an old crab," said Sadie. "No wonder he lives by himself."

That's what was missing from Mr. Rossi's silent, dreary apartment—family! But his life hadn't always been so different from hers, Rebecca realized. He had grown up with a big family, too.

"Maybe he wasn't always so grouchy," Rebecca said. "Maybe he's just lonely." Then she thought of something else. She dashed through the kitchen, stopping only to plant a kiss on her grandmother's cheek. She threw on her shawl, picked up the centerpiece, and bounded down the stairs.

Mr. Rossi opened his door just enough to reach for the pails, but before he could close it again, Rebecca thrust her arm through the opening and handed him the decoration. "Merry Christmas, Mr. Rossi," she said.

Mr. Rossi pulled the door wide open and beckoned her inside. He took the centerpiece and carefully set it on a small table in front of the window. Rebecca thought his eyes looked moist, but

perhaps that was from his cold.

"*Bellissimo!*" he said. "You made this?"

Rebecca didn't know what *bellissimo* meant, so she wasn't sure if Mr. Rossi liked the decoration or not. "I-I made it at school," she stammered. "I hope you like it."

Mr. Rossi shuffled over to a chipped cabinet and opened a drawer at the very bottom. "You're a good girl to take care of birds while I was sick," he said. "And you found my little Pasta, with her new family. Not many kids around here would do favors for me." He took a cloth bundle from the drawer

66

carefully unrolled two sparkling blue glass candlesticks. He handed them to Rebecca.

"I know you don't celebrate Christmas," he said. "But you light candles for Hanukkah. These belonged to my wife, a long time ago. I want for you to have them. You can light candles and enjoy them as she did, yes?"

"Oh, Mr. Rossi," Rebecca gasped, "they're beautiful." She looked at the old man and thought she saw a wisp of a smile. "*Grazie*," she said.

Rebecca stepped outside and closed the door with a soft click. Snow capped the graceful arches of the streetlamps and coated the stoop and the carved lion heads over the doorway. Even under the blanket of snow, she could still recognize the distinctive shape of each familiar thing in her neighborhood.

Rebecca turned to see Mr. Rossi lighting the tall red candle in the centerpiece. The window was bathed in its flickering glow. Mr. Rossi could enjoy his Christmas decoration from inside, and Rebecca could enjoy it from the outside.

Rebecca realized that Mr. Rossi wasn't at all the person she had thought he was.

Now that she knew more about him, Mr. Rossi seemed rather special. After all, how many people could turn an ordinary row house into a pigeon cove?

Rebecca held the glass candlesticks close and smiled. They might not be right for Hanukkah, as Mr. Rossi thought, but they were perfect for the Sabbath.

Close by, Rebecca heard the sound of laughing and singing. She was sure she heard cousin Max's voice booming out a song through the night. "Hanukkah, oh Hanukkah, come light the menorah…"

Uncle Jacob and Aunt Fannie came around the corner, carrying platters of food. Cousin Max was holding a big seltzer bottle and singing at the top of his lungs. Ana and her brothers were skipping and skidding through the slippery snow that covered the sidewalk.

"Happy Hanukkah!" Rebecca called gaily. "Welcome to Pigeon Cove!"

LOOKING BACK

HANUKKAH
IN 1914

A Hanukkah celebration

When immigrants came to America, they adopted
American traditions while trying to preserve their
own customs and beliefs. This was not always easy,
as Rebecca discovered. When she was growing up,
Christmas was the biggest holiday in America, just as
it is today. Because so many Americans celebrated
Christmas, it seemed like a national holiday rather

Many cities had public Christmas trees, like this one in New York City.

than a Christian one. Yet by 1914, America was home to millions of Jewish immigrants and their descendents who, like Rebecca's family, did not have Christmas as part of their religion.

In New York, the public schools were teaching young immigrants like Rose how to be Americans. Many teachers believed, like Miss Maloney, that celebrating the same holidays as other Americans would help the immigrants *assimilate*, or blend in and become more like other Americans. So in December, Christmas traditions were part of the school day, with the singing of carols, classroom Christmas trees, and projects where students made Christmas decorations to take home.

Some Jewish parents accepted this practice. They were very respectful of teachers and wanted their

A classroom Christmas party in 1904

children to learn American customs. But most Jewish families felt strongly, as Rebecca's family did, that being American didn't mean celebrating a religious holiday that was not part of their tradition. One thing that all Jewish families agreed on was that they loved celebrating Hanukkah.

Hanukkah began more than two thousand years ago, after a small group of Jews fought against a Greek king for the right to practice their own religion. For three years, they battled until at last, the king agreed

Cleaning the temple

that the Jews could follow their own beliefs. With joy, the Jews cleaned their temple and dedicated it for Jewish worship once again. To complete the ceremony, they needed purified oil to light the altar lamp, but they could find only one small vial of oil, just enough to last one day. As the story is told, the lamp miraculously burned brightly for eight days, long enough for the Jews to prepare more oil.

menorah

To remember the triumph over the king's decree and the miracle of the oil, Jews celebrated a holiday each year. They called it Hanukkah, which means *dedication* in Hebrew. Each night for eight nights, they lit oil or candles in a special lamp called a menorah. They ate foods that were fried in oil, to remember the oil that burned for eight nights. This Festival of Lights, as Hanukkah is also known, reminds Jews of the importance of religious freedom.

In the old country, Jews in Russia and other parts of the world observed Hanukkah as a minor holiday on the Jewish calendar. Just as they had done in ancient times, they

In Russia, children received coins for Hanukkah like the ones at right.

HG.

lit menorahs and ate fried foods. They also gave to the needy and gave children a few coins, called gelt, as a special treat.

After Jewish immigrants settled in America and found greater freedom and a more comfortable life, Hanukkah became a bigger holiday, with festive family gatherings. Children sang Hanukkah songs, enjoyed traditional foods such

latkes

as latkes, and played dreidel games. Family members also began exchanging small gifts, in addition to giving to charity.

dreidels

In Rebecca's time, shopkeepers encouraged people to give lots of gifts on Hanukkah and Christmas, just as they do now, because more gifts meant more shoppers in their stores.

Shoppers in 1914 were flocking to a special kind of store—the department store,

Many department store chains were founded by Jewish businessmen, such as Joseph and Lyman Bloomingdale.

This patriotic menorah shows the Jewish people's affection for their adopted homeland.

where people could buy almost anything they wanted in one place. Many of today's largest department stores got their start back in the late 1800s. With the rise of department stores, both Christmas and Hanukkah—and holiday shopping—became bigger than ever before. Today, Jewish-American families still celebrate Hanukkah, as Rebecca's family did. And all Americans feel the same way Papa did— that one of the best gifts America gives its citizens is the freedom to celebrate their own holidays.

GLOSSARY

bellissimo *(bel-LEES-see-moh)*—Italian for **very beautiful**

bubbie *(BUB-bee)*— **grandmother** in Yiddish

chutzpah *(HOOTS-pah; first syllable rhymes with "foot")*—the Yiddish way of saying **boldness, nerve**

dreidel *(DRAY-dl)*—in Yiddish, a **toy** marked with Hebrew letters and spun like a top; also, the Hanukkah **game** played with a dreidel

gelt *(gelt)*—a Yiddish word for money, especially **coins** given to children at Hanukkah

grazie *(GRAHT-see)*—the Italian word for **thank you**

Hanukkah *(HAH-nik-ah)*—a **holiday** to remember the Jews' victory in regaining their temple in Jerusalem; Hebrew for "dedication"

kugel *(koo-gl; first syllable rhymes with "good")*—in Yiddish, a baked **casserole** usually made with noodles or potatoes

latke *(LOT-keh)*—the Yiddish word for a **potato pancake**

menorah *(men-OR-ah)*—a Hebrew word for **candelabra**

nosh *(nosh)*—to **snack,** in Yiddish

shammas *(SHAH-mes)*—the **ninth candle** on the Hanukkah menorah that is used to light all the others; from a Hebrew word meaning "servant"

yarmulke *(YAH-muh-kah)*—in Yiddish, a **skullcap** worn by Jewish men to show respect for God

Author's Note

The Jewish calendar is based on the cycles of the moon, so on American calendars, Jewish holidays fall on different dates and days of the week each year. Sometimes they even occur in different months.

In 1914, Hanukkah began on a Saturday night. In *Candlelight for Rebecca,* the story worked better if the first night of Hanukkah fell on a school night, so I wrote the story with Hanukkah beginning on Friday. Some years Hanukkah does begin on a Friday, and I felt that changing the day of the week made a better story without spoiling the overall historical accuracy of the book.

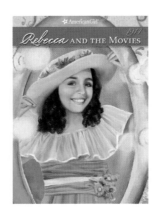

A SNEAK PEEK AT

Rebecca

AND THE MOVIES

When cousin Max invites Rebecca to visit his movie studio, she finds out what it's like to be a real actress!

Who's the doll-baby in the scrumptious hat?" said a sweet voice. An actress was walking up the hallway, carrying a brown wig with flowing ringlets.

"This is my cousin, Rebecca Rubin," Max said. "Rebecca, meet Miss Lillian Armstrong."

Rebecca smiled shyly and found she could barely speak. "Glad to meet you," she managed.

"Say, how would you like to see me turn from a real girl into a movie actress?" Miss Armstrong asked. Rebecca nodded, unable to say a word.

Miss Armstrong opened her dressing room door. Painted on the outside was a shiny gold star with her name in black lettering just underneath. Rebecca wondered if Max had a star painted on his door, too. Inside the small room, the wallpaper was printed with white lilies, and a vase of fresh lilies perched on the corner of the dressing table.

"First of all, you must call me Lily," said the actress. "We aren't very formal here." She pointed to an upholstered chaise longue. "Make yourself comfortable." Lily placed the wig on top of a coat tree and kicked off her shoes. She stepped behind a

Chinese folding screen and tossed her clothes across the top. A moment later, she emerged wearing a long flowered robe and settled gracefully on a stool at her dressing table. She opened a small case and lined up a row of jars and foil-covered sticks.

"Why do you have to wear all that makeup?" Rebecca asked politely.

"Without it, my face would photograph as a dark shadow. And after I make my skin pale, I've got to darken around my eyes, or they wouldn't show up at all. I know I look odd," Lily admitted, "but it all comes out bright and natural on film."

A light knock sounded on the door. *"Entrez!"* Lily called. A plump woman came in with an evening gown draped over her arm.

"My dress!" Lily exclaimed. She dropped her dressing robe on the floor and held her arms straight up in the air. Mabel pulled the dress over the actress's head. It swished down around Lily's dainty ankles, and Mabel began looping tiny buttons up the back. Lily strapped on a pair of delicate shoes that were more elegant than any in Papa's shoe store. Mabel picked up the clothes Lily had left strewn about. She clucked her disapproval, just as Bubbie would,

81

"Why do you have to wear all that makeup?" Rebecca asked politely.

but Lily didn't seem to notice.

"Shall we?" Lily asked, offering her arm to Rebecca. Together they walked toward the set.

"What happens in the movie?" Rebecca asked.

"Well, my parents have chosen a rich man for me to marry, but I don't like him. I would rather die than marry such a cad!" She changed her expression to a dreamy look and sighed deeply. "I'm secretly in love with the gardener. Of course, my parents wouldn't ever approve, and there's the plot."

Rebecca thought the story sounded a lot like real life. In fact, it sounded a bit like her own life. *Only in my case,* she realized, *it's movies I'm in love with—and my parents would never approve!*

Lily pushed open heavy double doors, and Rebecca entered a huge room with a glass ceiling. Light flooded across a stone patio with a carved railing and two stately urns overflowing with paper flowers. Behind the patio, the front of a mansion was painted on a large canvas backdrop. The mansion looked so real, Rebecca almost believed she could step inside. But the workings of the movie studio intruded into the illusion with wires, cameras, and rows of spotlights.

spotlight

83

Don Herringbone entered the studio, his face covered with pasty makeup and his eyebrows darkened, giving him a menacing look.

"There's my wicked suitor," Lily laughed.

"Lillian, my dear," he said. He took her hand and lightly kissed it. "You know you're in love with me!" Lily drew back coyly, her head turned to one side. Rebecca was fascinated. Was this part of their act?

Just then, Max walked over. He wore rough pants with suspenders buttoned over a loose white shirt, open at the neck. His hair fell in tousled waves under a soft cap.

"Ah, the gardener," Mr. Herringbone drawled, sounding haughty.

"Beware this scoundrel in fancy clothes," Max advised Lily.

Rebecca felt a shiver of delight. Were they all acting? Why, acting for a movie didn't seem any different from pretending with her friends. Rebecca could playact, too. She gestured toward Lily with a flick of her hand and spoke in a high voice. "I'm sure such an elegant lady knows her best suitor."

"You bet I do, doll-baby," Lily laughed.

Max coughed a little. "Come on, Rebecca," he

said, steering her away from the group. "Let's find
you a good spot to watch from."

At one side of the room, the actresses and
actors who had been on the ferry leaned against
walls, sat on chairs, and perched on props. "Welcome
to the garden," said an actress in a feathered hat.
"In case you can't tell, we're all lowly worms, just
waiting to be dug up. Extras like us just wriggle
around, hoping the Grand Pooh-Bah will pick us
for a scene—any scene, just so we can pay the rent!
Otherwise, it's move back in with Mama." The
other extras groaned.

Another young actress glared at Rebecca. Her
lips were painted fire-engine red and her glossy nails
were long and tapered. "Are you competition, or just
visiting?"

"I'm just here to watch," Rebecca assured her.
"I'm not an actress."

"Bet you'd like to be, though," the actress
replied. Rebecca squirmed under her steady gaze.
How had she guessed what Rebecca was thinking?
The actress turned to the other extras. "Watch out for
this one," she warned, pointing a long-nailed finger
at Rebecca.

READ ALL OF REBECCA'S STORIES,
available at bookstores and *americangirl.com*.

MEET REBECCA
When Rebecca finds a way to earn money,
she keeps it a secret from her family.

REBECCA AND ANA
Rebecca is going to sing for the whole school.
Will cousin Ana ruin her big moment?

CANDLELIGHT FOR REBECCA
Rebecca's family is Jewish.
Is it wrong for Rebecca to make a
Christmas decoration in school?

REBECCA AND THE MOVIES
At the movie studio with cousin Max,
Rebecca finds herself in front of the camera!

REBECCA TO THE RESCUE
A day at Coney Island brings more
excitement and thrills than Rebecca expected.

CHANGES FOR REBECCA
When Rebecca sees injustice around her, she
takes to the streets and speaks her mind.